AN ARCHIVE OF HUMAN NONSENSE

Jason Rolfe was born and raised in Southwestern Ontario. His work has appeared in numerous online and print venues, including *Sein und Werden*, *Pure Slush*, *Cease Cows*, *Apocrypha & Abstraction*, *The Journal of Experimental Fiction*, and *Black Scat Review*. His first collection, *An Inconvenient Corpse*, appeared as number 30 in Black Scat Books' Absurdist Texts and Documents Series (Black Scat Books, 2014). He regularly contributes to Black Scat Books' online journal, *Le Scat Noir*.

SNUGGLY BOOKS

THIS IS A SNUGGLY BOOK

ISBN: 978-1-943813-29-2

JASON ROLFE

AN ARCHIVE OF HUMAN NONSENSE

Snuggly Slim no. 8

THE ARCHIVE

O N the day his wife left him, Ernst Sieber met the count for coffee at a small café on Leopoldstadt. The café sat across from the public house frequented by Gustav Anschutz and his friends, and offered the two state policemen a broad view of the street in both directions.

The proprietor brought them coffee. Ernst thanked the man, but in truth he barely noticed him. His thoughts were focused on the count. Sedlintzky was not the partner he had anticipated when Metternich requested his transfer from the public to the state police branch. Sedlintzky was the chancellor's son-in-law, and as such had run the Habsburg Police Ministry since 1815. Sedlintzky was everything Ernst wasn't. He was a handsome man with a good name and an even better bank account. Where Ernst struggled to pay his debts, Sedlintzky had money to spare and often spent it on the frivolous fads and fashion of the day.

Sedlintzky neither took nor appeared to notice the coffee. Instead, he studied Ernst's earnest features. "You came highly recommended," he said. "I do not see it myself, but I must trust my good friend's judgement. You do know whom I am referring to, do you not, Herr Sieber?"

"I assume you are referring to the chancellor," Ernst replied. He loathed Sedlintzky's arrogance but knew better than to loosen the chains of sarcasm.

"Chancellor Metternich and I are close friends. We are, in fact, family. You would do well to remember that, Sieber. We share social circles you are not privy to. Our blood is blue. Yours is, of course, white. Clearly white despite your insistent hope that it is tinted blue."

"I am confident in its redness, Herr Sedlintzky."

"And I am confident that if your blood contained any tint, Sieber, it would be brown. Do you know why that is?

"Because I am full of shit, sir?"

Sedlintzky smiled. "I would suggest that sarcasm will get you nowhere in life, but what would be the point of that? You are not going anywhere in life regardless."

Ernst bit his tongue. He had learned very quickly that exchanging barbs with Sedlintzky offered little challenge and even less financial benefit. If he meant to get ahead in life he would need to endure the world's Sedlintezkys.

He returned his attention to the people on the street. If streets were the city's arteries, the people were Vienna's blood. He watched the blood flow for several minutes before Sedlintzky again interrupted his thoughts.

"Is that not Anschutz?"

Ernst followed his gaze across the crowded street. There, Gustav Anschutz stood, engrossed in conversation with a short, slightly rotund young man wearing wire-rimmed glasses.

The two detectives rose and left the café. "Follow Anschutz," Sedlintzky said. "I will follow the other."

With that, the two men went their separate ways. Ernst felt Sedlintzky's absence instantly. It felt as though a weight had been lifted from his shoulders, and he shadowed Anschutz with a noticeable spring in his step. Perhaps Sedlintzky's blood was blue, but his mind was a dull, dead grey. He could not see anything beyond the obvious, and even that took a great deal of coaxing. He was Metternich's son-in-law, however, and as such required very little wit and less wisdom to work his way up the chain of command. Ernst had come to suspect that until men like Sedlintzky ceased to be, men like Ernst Sieber would, rather than ascend the chain of command, forever be shackled by it. It made the chancellor's decision to transfer him from the public to the state police branch all the more perplexing. It was while serving as a public policeman back in 1814 that Ernst had thwarted an assassination attempt on Metternich's life, and it was as a public policeman that Sieber felt he had done his best work. Where the state police served the chancellor's desire to control thought, the public police served Vienna.

Ernst followed Anschutz through the city's winding streets, past public houses and private homes, down alleyways and broad, life-lined avenues. His days as a public policeman gave him an advantage over almost anyone else. He knew the streets intimately.

Following the affair, Vienna became his obsession. Ernst buried (some say lost) himself in the bright, broad streets and darkly shadowed alleys that together comprised the City of Music.

Gustav Anschutz unwittingly led the brooding detective to a small public house topped by a large red rooster. Ernst sat back and waited, watching as the young artist knelt and removed a key from beneath a loose cobblestone. Anschutz quickly slipped inside and shut the door.

Ernst fought the urge to cough. Unwilling to reveal his presence, the detective buried his face in the folds of his coat and tried to muffle the sound. The action be-speckled the inside of his coat, scarlet-black proof of the infection that troubled his weary lungs. He wiped his mouth on his sleeve and waited.

Forty minutes later Anschutz reappeared. He locked the door and placed the key back beneath its unmarked headstone before wandering back up the alley toward the Stephansplatz. Ernst watched him leave. He waited another ten minutes before approaching the Red Rooster.

Inside he found all the accoutrements of a public house, from a well-equipped bar to numerous stools and chairs. On the wall opposite the bar he found the fading words *Vivat es lebe Blasius Leks: Zur Unsinniade—5ter Gesang* encircling two figures, both men, one of whom no doubt represented the strange seal's focal point.

Ernst left the painting, delving deeper into the Red Rooster's interior. At the back, behind a series of wooden crates and what appeared to be a makeshift stage, he found a relatively new yet well-worn pianoforte. He moved quickly past it. Along the tavern's back wall he found a small writing desk, around which the floor was stained ink-black and littered with loose scraps of paper. Atop the desk he found a small stack of handwritten newsletters entitled *The Archive of Human Nonsense*. He picked one up. It was dated 17 April, 1817—eight months previous—and had been hand-penned in German running script. From front to back the small newsletter was eight pages long. It opened with a list of names, twenty-two in all, and closed with a watercolour picture of a giant red rooster. Aside from the names and the watercolour, the newsletter contained several humorous and off-colour texts spoofing Vienna's political establishment, her social mores, scientific discoveries, art, drama, and literature. In that single issue Ernst found enough evidence to condemn the authors to whatever ill-fate Metternich saw fit to deliver them to.

It must be understood that under Metternich, the Habsburg Empire had undeniably been transformed into a stifling police state. A word was not spoken within Vienna's walls that went unheard by the state police. Ernst worked for the branch of the Police Ministry responsible for the censorship of unorthodox thought. Since the ascension of Metternich, Vienna had been cloaked in an atmosphere of political repression and suspicion. The war against the French had, in essence, become a war against ideas. The Emperor simply did not tolerate the free expression of opinion. Metternich had once reiterated the Emperor's words in a speech at the Police Ministry, suggesting that the "cult of liberty" had gained so much ground that the "ordinary arrangements for peace and security" were woefully inadequate. "We must," Metternich said, "set all forces in motion for the good of the state, in order to convert those in error and to wipe out through effective countermeasures, all dangerous impressions that might have been instilled in any class of subjects by sneaking agitators."

Ernst did not understand the chancellor's way of thinking. In his mind, so long as Austrians had some dark beer and a little sausage, thoughts of revolution would never enter their heads. Still, based upon his fear of subversive societies and pro-revolutionary movements, the Emperor had restored capital punishment. Under Metternich, the state police did not limit their surveillance to genuine revolutionaries. They were sent everywhere in search of the slightest hint of unorthodox ideas among the citizenry. The chancellor's suspicion of intellectuals was such that many Viennese citizens avoided higher education for fear of their futures. "Our people must be protected from the poisonous aspirations of self-seeking seducers, and from the dangerous illusions of crazed heads," Metternich once told him. Ernst opposed the systematic use of brutality and terror in the enforcement of censorship and the suppression of ideas. At times he used the possibility of arrest, the loss of one's job, and the threat of force as a deterrent, but he more frequently plied his trade using sausages and dark beer.

He read through the newsletter twice, knowing full well that if the chancellor learned of its discovery the men who wrote it would be harshly dealt with. Although Metternich would exile the authors, Ernst recognized the double-meaning of the word and knew their bodies would likely be buried in unmarked graves outside the city walls. The lack of justice would be swift.

The names the document contained were clearly aliases. The names Goliath Pinselstiel and Kratzeratti Klanwinzi suggested the men might be painters, perhaps responsible for the watercolour at the end of the newsletter and the strange mural on the wall. The similarity between the names Blasius Leks, Chrisostomus Schmecks, and Damian Klex suggested the three were related in some way, while others remained somewhat mysterious. Quanti Verdradi, for example, could describe virtually every blue-blooded member of the Viennese government while Sebastian Haarpuder suggested the vanity prevalent in that same class. The name that caught and held his attention appeared at the top of the list, beside the word 'editor'. Schnautze clearly identified the man behind it.

Schnautze was an imperfect anagram of Anschutz.

SEBASTIAN HAARPUDER

"MAY I help you?"
Ernst's head snapped around. He had been so lost in thought that he had failed to notice Anschutz's return. "State police," he replied, for lack of anything better to say.

"And how are things at the Police Ministry, Herr . . ."

"Busy," Ernst said, declining the invitation to share his name.

"I do not doubt it! It cannot be an easy thing, keeping us in check, Herr Detective. I must confess that finding you here, rifling through my things, has left me feeling a bit uneasy myself. After all, I am not accustomed to visits from the Inquisition! Have you always made house calls?"

Ernst admired the man's honesty. There were many who compared the inquisitiveness of the state police to the invasiveness of the Inquisition. Were it Barcelona perhaps he would have frowned upon Anschutz's impudence, but as they were in Vienna and as he himself was an admirer of satire, Ernst ignored it. Instead, he focused on the watercolour hanging above the pianoforte. "Can you tell me the artist's name?" he asked.

Anschutz smiled up at the painting. "Ah yes, my dear friend Hoechle painted that as a gift on my last birthday. Johann Nepomuk Hoechle. If you are interested in acquiring his work, or perhaps employing his services, I would be happy to send him your way, detective . . ."

Ernst nodded thoughtfully and said, "I may have you do that, sir. I have seen similar work. I thought perhaps this piece was done by the same. Tell me, Herr Anschutz, are you familiar with the work of Goliath Pinselstiel?"

Anschutz's smile broadened. "Ah ha! An excellent guess, detective, but you are mistaken. While Hoechle is, in fact, Goliath Pinselstiel, this particular piece was painted by Kratzeratti Klanwinzi! Tell me though, how you became familiar with these two fine young men."

Ernst took the newsletter from his pocket and placed it on the table between them.

Anschutz's smile never wavered. Instead he laughed lightly and offered Ernst a drink.

"Thank you, no," Ernst said. "You do appreciate, Herr Anschutz—or should I say Schnautze—the stakes with which you play."

Anschutz laughed. "You are mistaken once again, sir! I fear you've taken me for my dear brother Eduard! Eduard inherited the big snout. I have something much bigger in my genes!" At this Anschutz stood and bowed very deeply, saying, "I, Herr Detective, am the gentleman referred to in that document as Sebastian Haarpuder!"

Ernst frowned. Schnautze was a perfect anagram for E. Anschutz. Eduard Anschutz. Reclaiming the newsletter he said, "Very well then, I have managed to identify your brother Eduard, yourself, and Johann Hoechle. Can you provide the names of the other gentlemen on this list? I should speak with them before returning to the Ministry with this enlightening information."

Anschutz frowned. "My good man," he said. "We are harmless! I understand the need to protect the Empire, but what threat can be posed by a simple society such as ours? We are musicians and artists, not pro-revolutionary anarchists. If we wield any weapon at all, sir, it is our wit and, having read this newsletter I am certain you'll agree that, with few exceptions our swords are quite dull!"

"I need their names," Ernst insisted. "Your intentions and our perceptions may remain two vastly different things, and given my knowledge of the Ministry I can tell you truthfully which view will be the prevailing one when it comes time for judgement. I merely wish to warn your friends against further nonsense. They are, and shall continue to be, under our surveillance. I would hate for your good fun to bring about prison, banishment, or worse."

Anschutz appeared deeply hurt by the implication. His frown, however, quickly curled back into a smile and he said, "I will do better than give you their names, good sir. I shall introduce you to each of them personally. They are my good friends, after all. I would hate for them to think that I have ratted them out, and as I am certain we are innocent of any and all crimes it would do well for you to meet them in, such as it is, their element!"

"Promptly?"

"Very," Anschutz replied. "Allow me to pour you a drink while we await their arrival!"

"They are coming here?"

"Tonight of course," Anschutz said. "It is New Year's Eve after all."

Ernst quietly considered the man's invitation. Liesel would assume the worst, of course.

Anschutz smiled again. "You are thinking about your wife. One might suspect, if you're not careful, dear detective, that you have a conscience. A conscience in most would be considered an asset, but in a member of the state police it can be a fatal flaw! Don't worry," he added with a condescending pat on Ernst's shoulder. "Your secret is quite safe with me. If others suspect your goodness, they shall not hear of it from me!"

He handed Ernst a drink. "To our blessed Insanius," he said.

"Who?"

"The god of nonsense, dear man. Drink up! Drink while our hearts still beat within our chests!"

13

FAÇADE (A FRAGMENT)

*F*ROM *the street the house maintains its grace, yet as Ernst steps through the ornate, arched gate and approaches the door, he sees the house for what it is—an old house, neglected, falling slowly but inevitably into decay. It is a house whose fading beauty will soon be lost to the perils of time. Despite his father's best efforts, it has never truly been noble, and its crumbling frame seems somehow befitting the marriage it entombs. Ernst feels mocked by his ancestral home. Although passers-by often stop to admire the building from the street, none see the caustic discomfort that exists beyond its opulent façade.*

His parents lived and died beyond their means, sacrificing everything to appearance, not so much for love of vain ostentation as from a adolescent need to fit in and thus participate, albeit falsely, in the grandeur of the court. While Ernst detested his father's shallowness, he had to admire the man's determined courage and elegance, his downright dandiness in refusing to submit to poverty. Ernst never shared their ambition. He never felt the overwhelming need to live up to one's rank, to cut a fine figure even if one had to perform miracles of ingenuity to pay one's most pressing debts. That was their desire, not his. They belonged to a class that employed cooks and maids, butlers and lackeys and lived their summers in Enzersdorf hosting parties and exquisitely refined rural balls, all without a penny for their debts.

The house is cold and dark. Since the affair, the fires Ernst lights each morning die out during the day and remain unlit until his return. He finds it increasingly difficult to recognize Liesel's presence in their home. It is the music he misses. The lieder she once sang and the echoing of the pianoforte through the narrow halls and vaulted ceilings of their home. The only echoes he hears now are the reverberations of the silence Liesel screams at him.

NEW YEAR'S EVE, 1817

"WAKE UP, Herr Kopf."

Ernst raised his wine-laden head and coughed. It took several awkward moments for the fit to subside. When it did he tried and failed to hide the flecks of blood that dappled his sleeve. "I am unwell, Herr Anschutz."

"Haarpuder," Anschutz replied.

"Herr what?"

"I am Sebastian Haarpuder," Anschutz explained. "The party, good sir, is set to begin. But first, your disguise."

Ernst looked at Anschutz. He was dressed in late Baroque style. His long, lean coat and matching waistcoat bore elements of decorative exuberance, a bright gild work that framed both sleeves and pockets and seemed inconsistent with their military inspiration. A periwig completed the ensemble, its brilliant whiteness highlighted by a tag which read, 'Extra Fine Hairpowder.'

"My disguise?"

Anschutz pulled him from his chair and all but dragged him toward the back of the room. "If you wish to observe our group at its nonsensical best you cannot simply stand there and stare at them. We are not a menagerie, my friend. We are an interactive display. You must participate! Besides which, I have the perfect costume for you."

"Less . . . enthusiastic . . . than yours, I hope."

"It is fitting."

"I should hope it fits."

"I meant appropriate," Anschutz said. He led Ernst into a small back room, one the detective had overlooked during his earlier exploration. The room, no larger than a pantry, contained a wardrobe and a small dressing table. It was dark and difficult to see even after Anschutz adjusted the gas-lit sconce. "Everything you need is here," he explained. "It is most fortunate we are similar in size, else you would be most uncomfortable. If you find that your wig needs powder, I do have some to spare."

"What did you do to me?" Ernst asked. "The wine . . ."

"Was strong and you drank far too much for your wits' liking. The unexpected nap will serve you well though, as tonight will undoubtedly bleed into morning. Listen! Others are arriving! Get dressed quickly. I will be waiting outside."

When Ernst emerged several minutes later, Anschutz looked him up and down and smiled. "You do look perfect, Herr Kopf. I knew you would. Yes, despite your dourness I do think you will enjoy our little group."

Ernst looked down at his costume. He found the periwig itchy to the point of distraction, but resisted the urge to scratch. He knew that once he started scratching he would be unable to stop. "Haydn?"

"Haydn," Anschutz said. "Perfectly so."

"Why Haydn?"

"Someday, Herr Kopf, you will look back on this moment and say, 'of course Haydn.'"

"Why Kopf?"

"Always the detective," Anschutz said. "Our code names are always plays on words. Yours, for example, has a double-meaning, neither of which you would appreciate without divining yours and Haydn's interlinked fates and knowing the English slang term for a policeman."

"I do not understand."

"Of course not! I admit that your costume and your name were my ideas, but you were drunkenly complicit during the entire affair."

"Affair?"

Anschutz laughed. "Really, Kopf. I meant our plans for the evening, your disguise. You wanted to observe the Society without tipping your authoritative hand, so I provided you with the means to do so, means befitting our beloved Nonsense Society. I am flattered you would consider the matter an affair," he added with a wink. "Imagine the scandal!"

"I would rather not."

"Lighten up, Herr Kopf! Enjoy yourself tonight. Find meaning in our madness!"

"I suspect we have different definitions for the word 'enjoy,'" Ernst replied. His eyes returned to the room around them. Slowly filling with costumed revellers, it now seemed odd and otherworldly. "What is this, anyway? Is it art? A performance of some kind?"

"I suppose you could refer to it as artwork, but its point is far more philosophical and far less meaningful. We mask the world so that we might reveal its true face."

"It's true face?"

"You speak like a policeman, and in your head perhaps you are one. But in your heart you are a poet. I know, Kopf. I have an eye for poetry."

"Absurd," Ernst said.

"Quite possibly so," Anschutz replied. "If I have an eye for poetry, my heart belongs to the absurd. You and I, we live together in this city and its surrounding world. Can you honestly tell me there is a point?"

"A point to what?"

"To any of it. To all of it! The world is nonsense, Kopf. Utter and undeniable nonsense! Admit it. You see more sense in nonsense than in the nonsense doled out by our priests and statesmen."

"I admit nothing of the sort," Ernst replied, taken aback by the man's perspicacity. His mind wandered back to the library and Liesel's last words, I won't be here when you come home. Was it nonsense, or would she really leave him? Generally reserved and intensely private, Ernst felt the urge to confide in his companion. "Do you honestly believe this world of ours is meaningless?"

"Not meaningless, dear man. Pointless. Supremely pointless. There's a difference, you know. There may not be a point to all of this," he swept his arms around dramatically, "but we can ascribe our own meaning to it, to everything we do."

"I find the search for meaning completely pointless," Ernst replied. "The question isn't why we're here, but rather why we stay."

"You mean why we don't end ourselves?" Anschutz asked, eyebrows raised. "Where is the fun in suicide, my dear Kopf? What joy can be found in self-destruction? You're missing the point of pointlessness altogether."

"Which is?"

"The freedom to find our own meaning."

"A pointless exercise," Ernst said.

"An incredibly absurd one, Herr Kopf, something far nobler and graced with human dignity than anything else we could do as a race."

"Noble? Really?"

"Ah," Anschutz exclaimed, glancing toward the entrance, "The Knight Cimbalom has finally arrived. I promised you introductions, my good man, and who better to start with than our beloved Juan de la Cimbala? Come with me."

Ernst followed him through the growing crowd. The name, if not the face, struck a chord. Cimbala, Cimbalom, seemed closely related to *cembalo*, the Italian word for harpsichord. Given the names Ernst had discovered in the newsletter it seemed a safe assumption that his first introduction was a musician of some sort. He was a short man with curly sideburns. He wore small, oval-lensed glasses and a brown suit. Two young women dressed in formal white and blue followed him into the room. Although the women were unfamiliar to him, Ernst immediately recognized the man as the person Sedlintzky had followed from the small café on Leopoldstadt earlier that day.

"A musician," he noted.

"You recognize our beloved genius then?"

Ernst sensed the uneasiness in his companion's voice and shrugged. "Of course." It was a lie, albeit a strategic one. Anschutz's discomfort suggested that the musician had a reputation worth protecting. "A prominent figure!"

Anschutz laughed. It was a pleasing sound. "You see," he said. "I knew you would fit in perfectly. Our rotund Cimbalom does indeed have a rather prominent figure!"

"I was not commenting on his physique," Ernst quickly pointed out, "but rather his standing."

"Indeed, Herr Kopf. He is standing in prominent position, but then Juan de la Cimbala does like to be the centre of attention. Come, introductions!"

With that, Gustav Anschutz, the self-titled Sebastian Haarpuder, stepped into the shorter man's immediate orbit and bowed deeply. "Good night, good knight!" he said. "And who are these two fine Graben nymphs?"

Ernst felt the biting gaze the two women gave Anschutz. The Graben had long been associated with prostitutes, an association that perhaps carried over to the mysterious Don Juan de la Cimbala.

"Babette and Therese," the stout man replied, brushing aside his friend's faux pas with a wave and a warm smile. Then, turning toward his guests, he added, "Do not be offended. Herr 'Powder was merely jesting at my expense."

"Absolutely!" Anschutz agreed. "My jokes are always at your dear friend's expense. I simply could not afford them without his patronage. But please, allow me to introduce a guest of my own! For this fine gentleman I have chosen the name Kopf."

The trio eyed Ernst's costume appreciatively. Along with a periwig he wore a fancy uniform with lace, embroidery and gold thread that broadened the smile on Cimbala's round face. "Haydn, sir. I applaud your choice!"

Ernst shifted uneasily in his suit. "I merely wore the costume Ans . . . Herr Haarpuder provided."

Anschutz bowed deeply. "I merely painted a portrait upon your canvas. We were just discussing the pointlessness of life, Herr Cimbala."

"Pointless, but not without meaning," Cimbala countered.

Anschutz looked at Ernst and beamed. "You see? I would wager that Herr Kopf has a weight of some sort upon his heart."

"Indeed," Cimbala mused. "You look troubled, Herr Kopf. Upset."

"Quite so," Anschutz agreed. "It has been my experience, Herr Kopf, that those who espouse life's pointlessness generally do so to appease their conscience."

"There is no point," Ernst said. "So guilt, too, is pointless. We are simply here and then, one day, we are not."

"We are what we do," Cimbala said. "What have you done?"

"Guilt is evident in your denial of meaning, sir," Anschutz said. "You seek to assuage it by denying meaning."

"It is not your affair," Ernst snapped.

Anschutz snapped his fingers. "An affair! You had an affair."

"It was meaningless."

"Perhaps it was," Anschutz said. "I suspect, however, that your adamant refusal to admit meaning is meant to counter your poor wife's tendency to ascribe a deeper meaning to it."

"There is always meaning," Cimbala added. "Perhaps the meaning is not yours, but it belongs to somebody and is no less valid."

Ernst shrugged and looked around the room, no longer willing to confide in his strange companions. "If you do not mind, gentlemen, ladies, I should like to observe your group before forming my opinion."

"Observe?" Therese laughed.

Babette frowned. "You sound like a policeman, Herr Kopf."

"Very astute," Anschutz whispered. "Our new friend is exactly that. A state policeman, in fact. He has come to see us perform."

"For what reason?" Cimbala said, evidently troubled by the revelation.

"He would know whether or not we are a subversive group," Anschutz replied. "He would judge us either harmlessly flamboyant or worthy of Metternich's grand inquisition."

"And you brought him here?"

Anschutz pressed a finger to his lips. "Tell no one else, dear Cimbala. You needn't fear. We are hardly a threat to the chancellor's empire. At our worst we're a threat to common sense! One night with us and I am all but certain Herr Kopf's report will liberate us from the Ministry's lofty suspicions."

"What does the big snout think?"

"Schnautze? I will let you know exactly what he thinks when, and if, he finds out," Anschutz said. "But first," he caught the bartender's attention with a flourishing wave, "let us drink to our health, our happiness, and to Insanius, the great God of Nonsense!"

The bartender promptly brought them a decanter. The decanter contained a clear liquid and was accompanied by five glasses.

"Obstler," Anschutz explained in response to Ernst's inquiring gaze. "Drink with us, Herr Kopf. Drink with us and you'll see the world through our studious young eyes!"

Anschutz led them through the first bottle, Cimbala through the next. By the time the five found a third they were sitting together on the floor at the centre of the swiftly spinning room. Ernst, whose attention had been drawn within their small circle looked outward for the first time in several hours.

It was then that he noticed they were no longer in the Red Rooster, but were on a street Ernst had not visited since the affair.

"Gretchen," he whispered, the name a drunken breath upon his fevered lips. Ernst reached out and grasped Anschutz's sleeve. "How is it that we've come here?"

"You brought us here of course."

"What better place to explore the world's nonsense than the Jaegerzeile," Cimbala said.

"Can we visit the Soothsayer?" Babette asked. "I do love hearing what he has to say!"

Anschutz smiled and offered her his arm. "But of course, dear girl! What would a trip to the Jaegerzeile be without a visit to Sebastian von Schwenenfeld's marvelous theatre?"

Ernst tried and failed to remember how and when they had crossed the city, from the Red Rooster to the Jaegerzeile in three bottles of peach schnapps.

GRETCHEN (A FRAGMENT)

*T*HE JAEGERZEILE *is nothing and everything Ernst remembers it to be. It is still, without question, a menagerie. The Viennese love of pageantry brought life to such streets, transforming them into fairgrounds where mountebanks, quacks, clowns, and exhibitors of trained beasts shouted one another down in an indefatigable attempt to attract curious passersby. There is something darker there now. The street he had savoured as a younger man has lost its innocence. The brightly painted posters have faded ever-so-slightly, the smiling faces offer hints of menace, a snarling, biting laugh that* *echoes in his memory. Unlike the trained beasts within the countless theatres that once lined the Jaegerzeile, Guilt remains an untameable creature.*

Ernst pauses before the crumbling ruins of an old theatre. A sign above the door reads, The Mechanical Theatre of Sebastian von Schwenenfeld. *Although some time has passed since their last encounter, he swiftly recalls the Soothsayer. Ernst tries the door and is surprised when it opens for him. The theatre lobby is dark, speckled only by the sunlight filtering through the filthy windows. An inexorable blanket of dust covers everything but finds new life in each of his uncertain steps. It dances in the dirt-filtered sunlight and swiftly brings an itch to Ernst's nose. He turns his head and sneezes, and when his eyes again opened he sees the automaton.*

It wears the pointed hat and ritual cloak conjurors and magicians once draped themselves in. Its long and wavy beard gives it a majestic appearance, despite the years of dust and cobweb blanketing it, and its expression is earnest. Ernst, Gretchen has said. Like yours.

"I don't believe our lives are predestined," Ernst whispers. "Why would I place any weight on this automaton's words?"

For the fun of it. Gretchen's words disturb the dust that sleeps upon the surface of his memory. "You always wanted fun," he whispers. "Nothing more and nothing less."

PIQUANCY IS THE SPICE OF LIFE

"ONE cannot spend the entirety of one's life at the opera," Cimbala said. "And even if mountebanks, puppet showmen, and trainers of performing monkeys solicit spectators in the open street, they must compete with the life of the street itself, which provides infinite opportunities for delight. Our dear friend Sebastian Haarpuder likes to wander, wide-eyed through these streets, ready to be amazed by everything he sees. For him, everyday life is an endlessly entertaining spectacle."

Ernst understood the street's appeal. From the behaviour of passers-by, the patter of cheap-jacks and quarrelling coachmen with their oft-surprising wealth of slanderous language to the pretty, barefoot flower girls in their many-coloured aprons, to the hawkers with their trays of trinkets and the rustling tumult of the open markets there were a thousand potential delights.

"For Sebastian, life is a perpetual holiday," Cimbala said, his voice intruding on Ernst's thoughts. "He is interested in everything. Why, just last week he insisted that we watch a parade of oxen being driven to the slaughterhouse."

Therese groaned. "Everyone wants to see the arrival of the oxen."

"And you do not?" Anschutz asked. His surprise seemed both innocent and authentic.

The allure eludes me. The whole city abandons workshop and counter, puts on its Sunday best and for no other reason than to watch the passing of the cattle with the secret hope that some untoward accident might add fresh piquancy to it."

"Precisely," Anschutz replied. "Piquancy is the spice of life!"

"It reminds me of that old theatre," Babette said. "What was it called, the one where people went to watch wild animals tear one another to pieces?"

Ernst nodded, but could not recall the name either. "It was destroyed by fire," he said.

"Fortunately so," Therese said. "It was a horrible custom."

"A very old one," Ernst noted, "so deeply rooted in the Viennese way of life that its horror no longer seemed . . . horrific."

Anschutz shrugged. "If one wants to watch wild beasts tear one another apart, one need only wait for the next war."

In the near distance someone screamed.

DEATH AND THE MAIDEN

THEY paused to watch a trained monkey dance along a tightrope tied between two rooftops. The creature's impeccable acrobatics delighted the crowd, and the success of its performance brought an almost human smile to its inhuman face. It leapt from its perch, landing with alacrity upon the stage below. Though small, the simple stage housed a table upon which slept several smaller than normal musical instruments. At the trainer's command, the monkey picked up a violin.

"Can it play Schubert?" Anschutz asked, much to the delight of the curious crowd.

"With the right teacher, this aristocratic creature can play anything."

"What a coincidence! Our performing monkey can also play Schubert!"

"May I?" Cimbala asked, reaching for a small parlour guitar. Both the trainer and the trained monkey acquiesced.

Cimbala quickly tuned the instrument and, without hesitation, began playing an acoustic rendition of the Matthias Claudius poem, *Death and the Maiden*. His voice was soft and solemn and, though he could not explain why, struck Ernst like a knife in the chest.

> Pass by, oh, pass by!
> Away, cruel Death!
> I am still young, leave me, dear one,
> And do not touch me.

"That was the maiden," Anschutz whispered in Ernst's ear, "and now Death's response."

> Give me your hand, you lovely, tender creature.
> I am your friend, and come not to chastise.
> Be of good courage, I am not cruel;
> You shall sleep softly in my arms.

"It is beautiful, but so terribly sad," Therese said. "Don't you think so, Herr Kopf?"

Ernst did not reply. He was thinking about Liesel.

The monkey, clearly unimpressed by Cimbala's sad song, discarded the violin's bow. He tipped the instrument sideways and, plucking it like a guitar, began playing a tune Cimbala clearly knew well, for the musician soon joined in, singing;

> I dreamt I was a little bird,
> And flew onto her lap,
> And as not to be idle,
> Loosened the bows around her breast.

"A sly little bird you are, Cimbala!" Anschutz said. Cimbala smiled and continued,

> Then I flitted playfully
> Onto her white hand,
> Then back onto her bodice,
> And pecked at its red ribbon.

"Be wary of his beak, Babette!" Anschutz warned. "It is far sharper than his wit!"

Babette blushed, but her eyes sparkled as she watched Cimbala's strange duet.

> Then I glided onto her fair hair
> And twittered with pleasure,
> And when I grew weary,
> I rested on her white breast.

The onlookers laughed, but Ernst watched the monkey play. To the untrained ear it was remarkable. He seemed to match Cimbala note-for-note, the uniqueness of the violin's plucked sound complimenting the weirdness of the music perfectly.

> There is no violet bed in paradise
> Which can supress that resting place.
> How sweetly I would sleep
> On her beauteous breast.

The monkey reclaimed his bow and finished with a flourish of showmanship that brought loud cheers and whistles from the assembled crowd.

Both man and beast bowed and shook hands. Cimbala smiled warmly and returned the guitar to its rightful owner before rejoining his friends.

"What an amazing little monkey!" Therese said.

Cimbala shrugged. "He was slightly off key and missed several important notes."

"I think she was referring to you," Anschutz said, clapping his friend on the back.

Therese blushed. "I wasn't!"

MADAM DENEBECQ'S METAMORPHOSIS PLAYHOUSE

THEY continued past St. John's Church. In the first booth on their left they spied a number of enormous and curious beasts, including a great number of fine parrots, whose bright colours attracted the attentions of Therese and Babette.

The owner, an elderly woman with silver-white hair and deep chestnut eyes smiled warmly when she saw Ernst. "It has been a while, Herr Detective. I trust love finds you well?"

Ernst shifted uncomfortably, but returned her greeting. "Friends," he said, "this is Madame Denebecq."

"Denebecq," Anschutz repeated. Then, as though a candle had been lit within the shadowed corners of his memory, he snapped his fingers and said, "The famous director of the Metamorphosis Playhouse!"

"My late husband," Madam Denebecq replied with an elegant nod of her head. "The playhouse was well known here a few years ago, but alas most have forgotten its magic."

"The memories are but misplaced," Anschutz assured her. He studied the theatre's crumbling façade and smiled. "Perhaps while our birds admire your birds we can explore the old birdhouse?"

Madam Denebecq smiled. "A show has already begun, but you have not missed much."

"A play?" Cimbala asked, evidently surprised to learn that the playhouse was still in use.

"Play, perhaps," Madam Denebecq replied, "but not a play. Theatrics, but far from theatrical, I am afraid. My husband's audience died with him. Mine is a much less so-phisticated crowd. The Metamorphosis has changed," she said, gently laughing at her own bitter joke.

※

Although the performance had already started, Ernst, Cimbala and Anschutz found three seats near the poorly lit stage. The actors were puppets, marionettes controlled from above by a series of strings. The characters on stage leapt and danced or tripped and fell at the whim of un-seen hands somewhere in the shadowed heavens of the old theatre. Their seats were close enough to see the sur-prisingly detailed features of the show's stars. Its puppet actors were short, childlike but thick, as though their di-minutive size had been the intent rather than the extent of their growth.

"They look like dwarves," Cimbala whispered.

One of the marionettes stopped and glared at them, it's crudely painted eyes narrowed by thin black eyebrows into a mien of contempt. Cimbala sank deeper into his seat and looked away.

Anschutz chuckled.

Ernst marveled at the marionette's lifelike response. Had the eyebrows shifted? Had the eyes truly narrowed contemptuously? Of course not, he thought. It was but a trick of the light, the flickering of gas-lit shadows in an unexpected breeze.

The performance continued. Two marionettes distanced themselves from the others. The woman wore the unmistakable white lace of a wedding gown. The man was clearly meant to be her bridegroom, though his scornful expression and apparent disinterest made it difficult to tell. The bride raised a small wooden flute to her red wooden lips and began playing a simplistic rendition of Haydn's forty-ninth symphony, 'La Passione,' Cimbala whispered.

The little bridegroom sank to the floor, its strings slackened by apparent indifference to the bride's music. While Ernst watched, the bridegroom seemed to change, to transform from something human into something far less so. "A rock," he noted.

"Cold and uncaring," Anschutz explained. "This is a Märchen, a German folktale."

"Have you seen it before?" Ernst asked.

Anschutz shrugged. "Maybe, I cannot say for sure. But the theme is common enough. Märchen often feature metamorphoses of men into animals and petrifaction."

"To what end?"

"Märchen were written for an unsophisticated audience, Herr Kopf. An audience perhaps untrained in the complexities of thought and speech. Their authors chose figures from the natural world to explain difficult concepts not understood by the less educated common man."

"So the metamorphosis . . ."

"Helped to explain the multiplicity of the human experience," Anschutz said. "The surrounding animals, plants and minerals served as symbols of transformation for man to explain his own problems."

Ernst frowned. "The man's transformation from bridegroom into, as you said, a cold and uncaring rock . . ."

". . . strikes me as particularly poignant given the audience."

"It strikes me as particularly coincidental, Herr 'Powder," Ernst replied.

"Meaning exists wherever and whenever we ascribe it. I merely wish to prescribe it to you!"

"You ascribe meaning where it does not exist. You attempt to prescribe it when it is not wanted."

On stage, the rock transformed back into a little bridegroom and stepped toward the three men. It's dark and brooding glare had narrowed even further, and its teeth were bare. "You will need a doctor's prescription if you continue talking over the performance."

"We are trying to elucidate," the bride added. Her voice was gentler but no less disturbing than her wooden companion's. "Do you think that because we are a small theatre troop we have no feelings?"

Anschutz smiled and opened his mouth to speak, but the puppet bridegroom raised its string-bound hand and said, "If you are about to comment on my associate's use of the word 'small' and our size, please stop."

The bride raised her hand, or rather, the unseen puppet master raised it for her, until it was level with her neck. "We have had it up to here with jokes about our height."

"Of course," Anschutz pointed out, raising his hand to his waist in a similar fashion, "that is only up to here on us."

"That's it!" the wooden bridegroom shouted, leaping off the stage and from his puppet master's control. He landed squarely on Anschutz's chest, sending him tumbling over the back of his chair. In answer to their friend's call, more than a dozen marionettes appeared from backstage and charged recklessly into the unexpected fray. Sebastian Haarpuder, though lost beneath a pile of wooden little people could be heard saying, "You are making a mountain out of a mole hill!"

Ernst and Cimbala each reached down and pulled their friend from beneath the furious puppets. Anschutz quickly scrambled to his feet, brushed the dust from his jacket and kicked one of the puppets back onto the stage. He reached down and grabbed his over-powdered periwig. "Do not," he shouted, "expect a very good review from me!"

Still enraged, the puppets chased the retreating men from Madam Denebecq's theatre into the swirling, crowded mass of the Jaegerzeile. Once there, Anschutz led them through a maze of wild animal cages, mountebanks and acrobatic monkeys until they reached the relative safety of St. John's churchyard.

The three men sat down with their backs against three headstones and laughed. Ernst shook his head incredulously. "Masterful performance," he said. "How those puppet masters managed that is beyond me, but it was well worth the price of admission."

"Admission was free," Cimbala pointed out.

"Precisely," Ernst replied. "Priceless."

Anschutz smiled and raised a curious eyebrow. "You believe the puppet masters were responsible for that performance?"

"Who else?"

Anschutz pulled a splinter from his chin and raised it, like a trophy, over his periwigless head. "Stranger things have happened to the Nonsense Society, Herr Kopf."

Ernst shook his head again, more adamantly than before. "They were dwarves, of course. Cimbala said as much. That explains the offence they took at your comments."

"I was certain you were going to tell us that it explained their short fuses."

Cimbala laughed, but Ernst simply continued shaking his head.

"As I was saying," Anschutz said, grasping the thread of their earlier conversation as though nothing strange had happened, "The man's transformation from bridegroom into cold and uncaring rock should strike a chord with you, Kopf. But petrification is not the important thing. Although we witnessed it in a slightly different, not to mention angrier form, it is the bridegroom's transformation back from rock to man that makes this particular Märchen so important."

"How so?" Ernst asked, still bewildered and slightly light headed by their recent experience.

"It symbolizes enlightenment," Anschutz explained. "Redemption perhaps, an important lesson learned."

"The redemptive power of striking your chin?"

"That was unscripted. I suspect that in their original script the little puppets intended for the bridegroom and his bride to wed and, most likely, live happily ever after."

"And why should I find this Märchen particularly poignant?"

Anschutz sighed. "Perhaps that angry little marionette should have struck you on the chin, Herr Kopf. Come, I can see the Mechanical Theatre from here."

THE MECHANICAL THEATRE
OF SEBASTIAN VON SCHWENENFELD

THEY found Therese and Babette standing beneath the arched entrance to Sebastian von Schwenenfeld's Mechanical Theatre. At the apex of the arch was simple clock. To its left was a mechanical figure, a herald draped in Hapsburg colours who, as they watched, struck the hour on twin bells. To the right of the clock stood death. At the bell's toll he raised both scythe and hour-glass and seemed to glare not down at Ernst but through him. Beneath the clock he read the words, *venio sicut fur beatus qui vigilat.*

I come like a thief. Blessed is he who watches.

The room beyond the arch wore the mask of another Viennese neighbourhood. It was one Ernst knew all too well. Life-sized automata stood in small, animated groups on the street and within the windows of his house. At least it looked like his house, although its asymmetrical rococo style seemed younger and somehow happier than the fading ruin he inhabited.

They walked down the artificial street, their eyes exploring each exquisitely precise mechanical detail with wonder. Where his companions no doubt saw strangely lifelike automata, Ernst saw the oddly mechanical neighbours he rarely spoke to except in passing. His neighbour's maid was pumping water from their well; old lovers and young couples were strolling the boulevard, and there in the parlour window sat Liesel. While the automata around her clicked and whirred with artificial life, she simply sat beside the silent pianoforte with her wooden head in her wooden hands.

Ernst looked away. His eyes soon found an old man beating a drum in time with the ticking of the clock. The room before them and the clock behind were somehow linked. Despite the oddness of the moment, Ernst still marvelled at the craftsmanship. He stopped beside Therese and Babette, both of whom were watching a group of gossiping washer-women, whose sharp tongues rivaled those of the aristocratic ladies sipping coffee on the second floor. Two mechanical children were playing on a swing outside. He recognized them by their clothes and the colour of their hair, but he could not remember their names. The swing kept time with the drumbeat and the ever-ticking clock.

Ernst looked back at his house, not at the parlour window but at the second floor and the balcony outside the library. At long intervals a young brunette appeared on the balcony. She paused with her elbows on the railing and seemed to smile at the world below. She was foul-mouthed and funny, and she was never his. Gretchen was never anyone's. She was her own.

"The mechanism which effects all this is made of very simple components," Anschutz said. His voice startled Ernst, who had all but forgotten his companions. "Spools, iron wires and such, all fitted together with the greatest care."

"For what purpose?" Ernst asked, his voice barely a breath.

"Whatever one works best for you, Herr Kopf."

They left the mechanical street and entered the theatre itself, its walls lined with clocks and mechanical pictures, and shelves over-filled with mechanical toys and snuffbox automata, intricate music boxes, pocket watches, and caged mechanical songbirds whose little tin chirps Ernst found increasingly annoying. They passed mechanical menageries that mirrored those they had seen outside, from dancing monkeys to crawling spiders and brightly painted parrots. The noise and the constant motion left Ernst feeling nauseous. It was not until they left the hall that he began feeling well again.

The nausea returned when Anschutz told them they were standing in the theatre's original lobby. Ernst looked up and saw the old Soothsayer staring back at him.

"It's been a while," it said. The soft warmth of its voice coupled with the subtle, whimsical curl of its smile startled the detective. "What? You did not think I would remember your past visits? I remember everything, Herr Sieber. I know all and I see all. At least that is what I say. Herr von Schwenenfeld makes no such claims himself. He considers my prognostications a novelty, an entertainment and nothing more." The automaton leaned ever-so-slightly forward. Its hand moved fluidly toward its mouth, shielding it from von Schwenenfeld's sight. In a whispered tone it added, "I am, of course, obligated to say that. Given the litigious, not to mention libelous claims made against my chess-playing prowess, my master is reluctant to admit the veracity of my claims. I can assure you that my insights are uncanny and certainly worthy of your consideration, Herr Detective, particularly where your wife's fate is concerned."

"What?" Ernst asked. "Herr von Schwenenfeld, your automaton mentioned my wife. What game are you playing, sir?"

The man jerked his head in Ernst's direction, but his eyes remained unfocused. There was coldness in them that belied the life they surely held. "Ask. A. Question," he said. His halting voice rang hollow.

"I believe I just did," Ernst replied.

"Please forgive my master," the automaton said. "Oration is not exactly his strongest suit. Perhaps I can explain. Several months ago, when first we met, you were accompanied by a young woman who, if I am not mistaken, was not your wife."

"Enough!" Ernst snapped, his eyes still locked on von Schwenenfeld's unfocused gaze. "You will end the charade sir, or I will have you arrested."

The man raised his arm in jerks and spurts and held out a small piece of paper. Ernst took the note and read it:

DO NOT BELIEVE HIM

"What does this mean?" he demanded. "Who should I not believe?"

The automaton rolled its eyes. "Not this again." It turned toward its master and scowled. The facial features shifted with an ease that Ernst found disconcerting. Unlike the man it was glaring at, the machine possessed human qualities that contradicted its artificial nature. "I thought we had moved beyond this."

With a sudden, twitchy and completely unnatural jerk of his head, Sebastian von Schwenenfeld turned away from the strange machination and began whistling a tune that sounded like a simplistic version of Haydn's 'Symphony #4 in D-Major.'

"Evidently not," the automaton said, not without a touch of anger in its far-too-human voice. It turned back toward Ernst and its scowl swiftly shifted into a warm, albeit awkward, smile. "I apologize, Herr Detective. My master and I apparently have an ongoing dispute into the validity of my fortunes. Should you doubt them, my man, please allow this brief but highly detailed demonstration of my talents."

Ernst looked from machine to man and from man to machine; no longer sure he could tell the difference. "Of course," he whispered, instantly regretting the decision to allow the game's continuation. Nevertheless he added, "Please do."

The automaton cleared its throat, a phlegmy sound that suggested a surplus of oil, or perhaps some phlegm-like substance in its artificial mouth. "Thank you. Please understand that the images I attempt to convey to you appear as fragments in my mind's eye. For example, when I look into your future I see two heads."

"Heads?"

"Skulls, actually. Two bleached-white skulls. I cannot say who they are, where they are or what role they play in your future. I only see that they are there." The machine closed its eyes for a moment. "There and not there. I have no idea what that means."

"Perhaps they symbolize death," Anschutz suggested.

The automaton shrugged. "Perhaps; I do see death in Herr Sieber's future. The two visions appear unrelated, however. The death is more immediate, the heads more indistinctly distant."

"Who's death?" Ernst asked. "What are you talking about?"

The automaton closed its eyes again. When it opened them, Ernst thought he saw small teardrops forming in the corners of each. "You do not believe."

"I am skeptical," Ernst admitted.

"Your head and your heart are at odds," the automaton said, "While your head remains faithful, your heart has sought to recapture lost youth."

"Who put you up to this?"

"Your wandering heart has hurt someone more deeply than you realize."

"Ah, the heart," Anschutz exclaimed, clapping Ernst on the shoulder. "You cannot live with it, nor can you live without it."

"You mentioned an association between death and our friend's affair," Cimbala stated, his melodic voice tinged with caution.

"So I did," the automaton agreed. "So I did, indeed. I cannot say more save that death hangs its hat on this man's hearth tonight."

"Nonsense," Ernst scoffed. "You are but a machine, a machine whose very veracity has been questioned by its creator."

"Who, this man?" the Soothsayer asked, pointing its mechanical thumb in von Schwenenfeld direction. "He is not my creator. Whether you believe in Him or not, you and I share the same creator."

Ernst laughed and shook his head. "If I believe in anything at all," he said, "it is that Sebastian Haarpuder and his friends have been feeding you your lines since this entire encounter began. I will not pretend to understand the slight-of-hand involved, but I know a hoax when I see one. And you, sir," he added, turning toward von Schwenenfeld. "What have you to say for yourself?"

The strange man stammered and steamed and slowly, jerkily, raised his arm again. In it Ernst saw a second piece of paper. When he removed it his hand brushed against von Schwenenfeld's. The lack of warmth sent a shiver up his spine. Regardless, he turned the small paper over in his hand and read it.

THE INTELLECT
IS ALWAYS FOOLED BY THE HEART

"François de La Rochefoucauld? That is all you have to say, von Schwenenfeld?" He dropped both squares of paper on the floor and left the theatre. The world outside seemed smaller, its creatures closer than before. Everything was still, not calm but unmoving, and alive with anticipation. It seemed to Ernst that everything, from the songbirds to the acrobatic monkeys stood awaiting his return. When he stepped outside the world began again. The birds sang, the monkeys tumbled and the bustling crowd moved in perfectly choreographed synchronicity. He paused, certain he could hear something else—not above the rehearsed din but beneath it—the hollow-tin sound of Haydn's 'Creation' played through a music box.

"Absurd," He said.

"Yes," Anschutz agreed.

"I knew passion once. When I was a younger man, a boy really, I chased it madly. I found that passion had no use for me, nor I for it."

"Your affair?" Anschutz asked.

"Her name was Gretchen. She was a neighbour, and my tutor. She was so unlike any other girl I knew. She smoked and drank and swore like a coachman, and she played the most elaborate pranks on people. Her parents and mine were close friends, they shared the same social circles and so these pranks were invariably played on people too pretentious to laugh. I suppose I loved her back then, before I understood how pointless that endeavour could be." He shrugged. "Nothing came of it. She married a much older man and moved away. I never saw her after that, aside from last spring.

"The affair was an experiment. It satisfied nothing more than my curiosity. I wished to learn what it was I had missed all those years ago, when she and I were young friends."

"Yet now you struggle with the consequences."

"It meant nothing to me, yet Liesel does not see it that way. Her heart clouds her mind."

"You have it backwards," Anschutz said. "The intellect

42

is always fooled by the heart. I have seen the guilt in your eyes and actions tonight. That suggests that your head has not yet convinced your heart that your words ring true. The world is pointless, but not without meaning. As I've told you, a pointless world gives each one of us the freedom to make our own meaning. In doing so we make decisions that affect those around us. We are what we do. We must live with what we've done."

"I fail to see the point . . ." Ernst began.

"Your wife . . ."

"My wife is not your affair."

"You say the affair meant nothing, but it meant something to Liesel, and if I am not mistaken, Herr Kopf, she means something to you."

"I can see it now," Cimbala agreed. "Our automaton is alive after all, Herr 'Powder!"

"Alive but not well. Go home, Ernst. Go home and mend your wife's heart."

"My investigation is not yet complete, Herr 'Powder," Ernst said, annoyed by the abruptness of Anschutz's dismissal. "Although you have done your very best to distract me from my cause, I have not forgotten my duty to the Police Ministry."

"Gustav," Anschutz replied.

"What?"

"Call me Gustav, Herr Sieber. I have run out of hair powder and you, my friend, have lost your Kopf. Your wife needs you more than the Ministry."

"And if she is gone?"

"Then you find another meaning."

43

I COME LIKE A THIEF (A FRAGMENT)

THE house is quiet. Through the drink-blurred darkness he sees the dead memories and cold keepsakes his wife once cared for. The fires are out and the house is cold. He climbs the staircase to the second floor. There is an old clock at the top. It has always been there, a ticking memory of the minutes lived beneath its relentless gaze. To its left is their empty bedchamber, draped still in the bright-but-dusty colours of wedded bliss. To the right of the clock is the library. As the clock tolls four the open door seems to glare, not down at Ernst, but through him. The room beyond its steadfast gaze is devoid of life.

"I come like a thief," Death whispers. "Blessed is he who watches."

CPSIA information can be obtained
at www.ICGtesting.com
Printed in the USA
BVOW08s1946200117
474056BV00001B/4/P